ISBN-13: 979-8-9988914-3-4

Cover design by: C. Holtorf

LONG, COLD RIDE

An Iron Way Story

C. Holtorf

Smokeshow Publishing

TUBA'S MORNING

Tuba woke to the chill of a fall Colorado morning. He was glad of the moose skin that covered his cot. It was a whole damn hide, minus the head, and more than large enough to shelter the youth's body at night without his feet sticking out the bottom. He had gotten it from Bill for his birthday, just a few months past.

Bill had reckoned then that Tuba was sixteen, and Tuba was inclined to agree with the old man. It was clear that Bill wasn't Tuba's natural father. For one thing, Bill's skin was several shades paler, but as the only parent Tuba had known, Bill was the only one likely to know his birthdate, or his age.

The skinny boy's teeth chattered in the brisk morning air as he swung his wiry legs over the edge of his small bed, pulling the big moose-hide over his shoulders like a cloak. Tuba stood and walked across the plank floor of his twenty-four foot shipping container to the shutter covering the room's one window, a long and narrow rectangle cut into the steel wall with a torch and covered with a plywood and leather shutter. It swung open, inward from the top, and a cold breeze rolled through the room with the sharp white morning sunlight. Tuba ran his fingers over the edge of the window, a rough melted weld, and a thin rime of frost clung to the outside. The leather flap kept the window sealed, nice and tight through even the coldest nights, and a small oil heater kept Tuba's room nice and warm. He hooked the flat wooden shutter to a hook in the roof with the tether that also served as the inside handle.

Looking out from the container's perch, third in a stack as many high, Tuba surveyed the lot.

Five ragged camps were arranged on the broken tarmac surrounding Bill's Trade Stop. One group had been there three days, fixing an axle on their caravan. Four travelers and a team of six mules ringed their big fire pit. Their broken caravan had weighed heavily on road-weary minds, and Tuba had made himself a nice bit of scratch since their arrival by keeping the mules out of their way and tended in a row of drafty stock trailers that served as Bill's rental stables.

Tuba had made a bit more at cards with the fuel traders that had set up across from them the next night. The older marks always trusted his young face. Something about his wide smile or the unkempt poof of hair that he usually tied back with a thong just reeled them in. The fuel guys mostly dealt in wax and soap. Candles and blocks, though they would occasionally bring rich rendered fuel-fat to Bill in big blue plastic barrels. Tuba knew one of their driver-bosses, Gob. The man was large, tattooed and profane, but good hearted and friendly enough. He taught Tuba three different hands of cards a few years back, even gave the boy a deck of cards to practice with.

Tuba had proven a sharp student, and he surmised that the big man had occasion to regret his efficient tutelage since. This time, the fuel boys had been a team of two that Tuba didn't recognize. One was a muscular dope that played poor cards, the other a younger guy who smoked a lot. Nevertheless Tuba had done well for himself, and had come away with a tank of gas for his stove and six fair sized slabs of good jerky.

Across the lot from the wax-wagon, a group of solid looking toughs in leathers were set up in three simple tents, the triangular forms made a sawtooth against the multicolored wall of shipping containers.

These were enforcers from the Iron Way, a large gang from the north that kept old I-25 cleared of debris and nuisance from old Denver to Cheyenne. They were strong, hundreds deep Tuba had heard, though they seldom spoke to him outside of strict business and trade.

Tuba looked again at the three big motorcycles they had ridden in on. Beasts that ran on kerosene or fat-fuel or something. They were loud, bedecked with leather and shining metal. Tuba had respect for the Iron Way, but he didn't know if he liked them too much. They didn't small talk, wouldn't play cards, and never tipped. Mostly they ignored him, moving around him like he was just some child, and not the son of their host.

The other two camps were just passing through, both had arrived the previous evening, bought a meal and space in the lot and then settled in close. These were traveling types. One couple was riding horses and the other, a loner with a wolfish looking dog, was on his own two feet. Tuba hadn't yet spoken to either party, but maybe he would get a chance before they left. He often enough did.

Beyond the lot was a small village of shored up RV's and mobile homes, long ago fallen into a permanent settlement just outside Bill's train-container wall. Tuba's eye flitted over the familiar few wood smoke plumes, and the folks there getting up with the sun. He had walked those cracked asphalt paths many times, when he and Bill pushed their food cart through the little village, five or ten years ago.

So few of them had anything useful to trade for the food and fuel Tuba and Bill had on the cart, it had been all the two of them could do to keep from giving their stuff away, these people had it so hard.

Most couldn't produce enough to trade, and Bill would let them get the better of him, just to bolster their spirits. It had been a long time since last Bill had fueled up the little cart though, and Tuba hadn't wandered back in among those sagging plastic and plyboard squats since. When they could, folks came to trade like anyone else, and when they couldn't they tended to stay outside the perimeter wall, in respect of Bill's reluctant shotgun.

Tuba turned back toward the bunk. The window was on the long wall facing east across the yard, and the morning sun streamed in with the chill breeze. He went to the shelves at the head of his bunk and took a heavy woolen hoodie from the topmost. Pulling this on, he cast the moose hide to the floor in a heap, changed into new trousers and then slung the big skin back onto the bed, where it belonged. Tuba then went to the back of his house where the privy was.

CAT JIM ARRIVES

Tuba was just finishing up his breakfast, half of a smoked trout on a slice of the rough bread that he and Bill baked four times a week, when Cat Jim arrived.

Tuba heard the cowbells on Jim's mule ringing from the edge of the lot just as he was taking his steel plate to the little mess bucket he kept in his room. He would empty it when he went down to see Jim and Bill. Even as he cleared up his breakfast, Tuba's mouth watered at the thought of the contents of Cat Jim's packs. The trout he just finished was a trade from Cat Jim, and Bill had often said that there was no better beer than what Jim brought down the mountain with his meat and furs.

Tuba had only had beer twice, and both times it had been from Jim's stash. Bill didn't look kindly on habitual drunks though, and Tuba respected the old man enough not to partake without his leave.

At one narrow end of Tuba's house there was a door cut into the short side of the shipping container. The original access had been welded shut on both ends, and a new, man sized hatch cut out of one side of the old door long ago, to make of the place a small apartment.

Tuba had rigged a large wooden plank just outside the door, and a curtain of canvas overtop, so that the air couldn't get in. This he slung open and then kicked the roll of chain-ladder out of the resulting hole. Twenty feet of chain and dowel cascaded to the hard packed dirt below, and Tuba clambered down the resulting ladder with practiced ease, even jumping the last few rungs in his haste.

The boy walked briskly, squinting in the bright morning. He popped his hood over wind-whipped hair and strode towards the low, wide building at the center of the lot. He did his best to pass near to the two newcomer camps. While the couple were engrossed in tying their loads up and shoving off, the loner was still in his tent, his big dog asleep across the door flap.

By the time Tuba got to the café at the front of Bill's lot, Cat Jim had already tied up, and was inside, enjoying a cup of Bill's boiled coffee.

Jim smiled when Tuba entered, the long string of bells that hung on the door jangling as the youth pushed it wide. Bill turned to the pass-through shelf behind his counter and took down a breakfast of eggs, potatoes and a fried chicken leg. Jim nodded and Tuba gathered that he had ordered one of Bill's specials. Bill turned again to a battle scarred coffee urn almost as tall as himself and filled a cup, passing it to Tuba across the battered counter.

"You sleep well?" He asked.

"Yeah, it was OK. That moose keeps me really warm." Tuba replied.

"Cat here brought a raft of meat down off the hill, and two ponies of ale." Bill said.

Tuba smiled, Bill liked the ale Jim brought down from Abbey Farm, and Tuba liked just about everything else. He planned to ask Jim to take him up next year, when he was just a little older. Tuba's world was very small, and tended to end just near the edge of the wall of shipping containers that Bill and the Iron Way had built in a stalwart ring around his little slice of cracked-asphalt paradise just north of a moldering polyethylene slum. Jim was an old friend, though, and Tuba was sure he would take him back up to the farm when he asked. Next year, maybe.

"I already ate, Bill." said Tuba "I was thinkin' about some furs though." This he said looking to Jim, who smiled and replied "I brought a bunch, kid, you looking for a cat? Because I've got two marmots and a dog, too."

Jim looked over at Bill, who had glanced their way in surprise. "We lost a stud last month, kennel cough we think, but no one else in the pack has it. It's a good hide anyway, and don't worry, the meat is all coney and squab this time."

Tuba laughed. "A few cats will do, but I'll have a look at your marmots too, I have some good trade." Tuba had a small lockbox in his room that he kept his best barter in. Today it held a small flask of drinking alcohol, won at the card game with the wax traders the previous night. Tuba also had a middling sized pocket knife, oiled and sharpened by his own hand over long hours, and a pair of reading glasses. The last two were gleaned from the lot after various passers-through had moved out. He thought he could swing three, maybe four cat furs from Jim with this and he was looking forward to a new hat for the coming winter. It snowed at Bill's every year, and the frost on his windowsill this morning said that it was coming time to bundle up.

"I've got to tend to the newcomers, and see what we can get from them before they move on." Said Bill. "You two get along, right?" He said, smiling.

"Yeah, we'll be fine." said Tuba and Jim together. And Bill left, the front door bells jingling.

TRADE BAR

"**S**o, about those furs," Tuba began, but Jim cut him short. "Bill says you plan on coming up to the farm next summer." It was a statement, not a question.

"Yeah." Tuba replied, warming. "I want to learn to tan and brew. Bill says he just ain't the guy to teach me, but that's what you guys do up at Abbey, right?"

"Yeah, among other things." Jim replied. "Even in summer, life at Abbey Farm is hard if you go for full- share."

By that Tuba knew he meant privileges. Abbey Farm was a small stronghold up in the mountains, just behind the Front Range. They were self-sufficient, more or less. They sent Jim or a few others out to trade for luxuries time and again, but even that was supplemental to their keep. Tuba didn't know how long the Farm had been there, or how Jim had come to live with them.

Tuba was about to ask these questions when Bill's door swung open behind them, the long lanyard of jangling bells announcing the arrival of the loner Tuba had seen earlier, and his dog, who patiently waited at the threshold as his master, a swarthy young man held the door open.

"Usted tiene café?" the man asked, and followed more slowly with

"Can my dog come in with me, por favor?"

Tuba rose from his stool and went behind the counter to get the man one a mug, and then proceeded to fill it with coffee from the big stainless tank.

"Aqui esta café. Usted negociar?" Tuba asked. His Spanish was not perfect, but he had grown up watching Bill trade with everyone that came through, regardless of language or creed. Tuba had learned early that these things were above all, barriers to trade out here, and those that couldn't or wouldn't trade, died in the harsh wilderness between the settlements, alone.

The young man smiled broadly, showing spotty teeth, and pulled a dusty canvas backpack onto the long Formica counter.

"Tengo tobacco y marijuana" said the young man, and brought several folded paper boxes onto the counter. Jim's eyes smiled.

The young trader continued. "Tengo un poco de chocolate, tambien. Mi nombre es Rico." "I don't speak any Spanish, but I know what he's got! Can you help out Tube?" Jim said.

"Yeah, brother, no thing." Said the youth, reaching back to tie his hair into a rough pony with a length of knotty leather pulled from a pocket. "What should I tell him you have in trade?" Turning to Rico, he began "Soy Tuba, y mi amigo, Jim. Jim quieras negociar para su cigaros del mota."

Rico nodded and opened a few of the boxes he had lain on the counter, each contained a neat row of tubes of tan leaf, dry green herbs poking from the ends. He gestured to Jim suggestively and Jim took one of the slender joints from its box and sniffed at it appreciatively before dropping it back into the carton and taking his own leather satchel from the floor. He pulled a few objects of his own onto the counter.

In a few moments, a solar calculator, a cat fur and a grey-bladed knife that Tuba knew had been forged up at Abbey joined Rico's little cartons on the bar. Rico eyed the knife appreciatively. It was good work, the thick blade was almost two inches wide, maybe seven inches long, and only slightly curved to the tip. A curious figure was cut into the flat of the blade at the hilt, a sort of chain of three interlocking simple shapes. The first was a square, the second a triangle and the third another square. Jim noticed his attention and pointed the detail out.

"This is the maker's mark, sort of a signature. Said Jim. Can you tell our friend that this knife was forged where I live? By an artist named Samuel."

Tuba turned to Rico and did his best. "Aquí está el nombre del artista. Mi amigo le conoce. Es bueno." Rico smiled again, and nodded briskly, pushing two of his containers towards Jim and pointing to the knife.

Tuba watched closely, there was something magical to him about the transient value of things, how something small to him here could be a fortune to someone on the long road, or living on the mountain.

No doubt there was no shortage of ale or meat up at Jim's farm, but down here Bill and Tuba relied on trade to offset their meager food supply, and fuel merchants to keep the trade–stop warm and lit in the bitter winter nights. Travelers were often glad to give a little just to set up camp on the level asphalt inside the walls, behind a solid gate and in the company of others. Bill offered hospitality to just about anyone, and as a result enjoyed a good reputation with most regular traders along the old Interstate, as well as with the Iron Way, the powerful road gang based up north, in Wyoming.

As Tuba watched, Jim wrapped the knife up in the cat skin and tied the bundle with another strip of leather from a coat pocket.

He pushed the package over to Rico and pointed at the remaining boxes. "A little tobacco too, amigo?" He asked. Rico looked over at Tuba who said "Un poco de los otros cigaros?"

Rico nodded, understanding, and fished five similar cigarettes from another box. He added a small chunk of the chocolate as he put his cartons away and this he gave to Tuba with a smile and thanks. Tuba thanked him as well and Jim pocketed all save one of the joints and one of the cigarettes.

Tuba poured all of them another cup of coffee and they were just finishing this when Bill returned through the jangling front door. He had two others with him, the fuel traders, Tuba saw as they walked in behind Bill.
"Hoy, Rico!" said Bill, recognizing the small man at the counter.

"Ola, Bill." Said Rico warmly, "Estaba a punto de irse, yo le veré la vez próxima."

"That's bien, Rico, I'll see you next time." Turning to Rico's big dog Bill said "You too Blanco, viaje en paz." Rico smiled at this and spoke in labored English. "It is a long road."

"Vaya con dios." Said Bill, and at this Rico swung his bag onto his shoulder and took up Blanco's lead, heading out the door.

The younger of the fuel traders held the door for the man and his dog, and nodded amiably to Rico as he left. He was older than Tuba by a few years, but younger than Jim, and far junior to Old Bill. The older man was the one that Tuba had taken to the cleaners at cards the night previous, but he was in good spirits today.

"Tuba, Jim, I'd like you two to meet Doherty here, and the young man at the door is Julius. Did I get that right?" The last to the kid at the door, who nodded, coming forward to sit at the counter with his companion in the stool Rico had occupied a moment before.

Tuba smiled at both of them, having met them the night before. They gave him a cursory smile, but it was clear to Tuba that most of the previous night had been a drunken blur to the two men. He hoped they wouldn't be too angry about the gas.

"I would love a cup of your coffee, Bill." began the one named Doherty. "Julie and I ran out night before and we just can't get the engine started without a good cup. You good for it?" at this last the one called Julian laughed.

"You boys are welcome to the same hospitality I show anyone here." Said Bill, and continued as he drew two cups from the urn behind the counter. "Our business was fair and good, I thought, don't you boys think?"

Doherty nodded briskly, saying "Yeah, yeh, that's good trade we cut. No offense meant, Bill. We ain't with the 'Boys down south. They're dwindlin', what it's worth. What with the 'Way and all."

"Yeah, I reckon so." said Bill with a private smile. "So, will you two need help shifting the cargo?" This last he said arching an eye toward Tuba, who knew work when it was being assigned.

"I'd be happy to help you guys out, if you need it." The boy began, but he was quickly cut off by Doherty shaking his shaggy head.

"Nah, we're good." The big man said. "The boss would be pissed if he heard we let your guys touch the goods anyway. I'll kick down a few of those little white gas tanks if you fix us brekkie while we work, though, how 'bout that?" Doherty smiled in what Tuba assumed he thought was a friendly way, but the man's crooked teeth made the smile into a leer.

Bill took it well enough though, asking the two if chicken was alright, and then going to the back to fix some potatoes, yard-bird, and eggs in the kitchen. Tuba had heard that when Bill had come to the trade- stop, it had been only the hull of some 21st century diner, but the kitchen had been more than less intact under the debris of years. Tuba had been a baby then, and didn't know life outside of Bill's thirty foot wall of tractor-trailers, but sometime before then, Bill had been a cook, and so, it seemed, he had remained one.

The two men nodded at Jim and Tuba and left, presumably to unload the goods Bill had negotiated for while Rico and Jim had been making their trades. Jim looked at Tuba and picked up the joint he hadn't packed away. "You smoke this, Tube?" he asked coyly, then called towards the kitchen, "Hoy Bill! You wanna puff this jay?"

Bill appeared in the door shortly, the savory smell of a chicken fry up wafting from the grill behind him.

"No, man, that's ok." He said, then, looking over at Tuba "That stuff don't come through often, boy. Don't take too much a liking. You hear me?" He raised an eyebrow and Tuba looked at his feet. "Yes sir. Don't you worry about me."

Bill went into the back and Jim patted at his pockets until he found a brass tube. With a flip of the hinged portion, the cylinder became a brass handle, topped with a wick and flint-wheel as Tuba watched, and Jim spun this wheel with his thumb sending a shower of sparks onto the wick. Tuba laughed.

"Your firelighter is tricky!" he said, giggling. Tuba had never seen a handheld firelighter, unless you counted the sparking button on his gas stove, or the larger versions on the stoves in the kitchen in the back of Bill's kitchen.

Jim looked through the flame at Tuba, "Made this up at the farm too. Well, I didn't, but a friend did. Which reminds me, you and I have to talk." At this he lit the joint, and passed it to Tuba. "If Ol' Bill says it's alright, I want to take you up to Abbey Farm come the new year. Just for a while. What do you think?"

Tuba smiled, and took the joint that Jim held out to him. He had only smoked a few times before, and the last time the herb had been mixed with rough tobacco and he had choked for half an hour. This time though, the marijuana was smooth and strong. The bright resinous flavor pulled his cheeks into a grin, and he didn't feel obliged to stop it, especially since Jim had brought up the idea of taking the boy up to the farm at the start of the next season.

"So, here's the bargain," Jim began, as Bill came back to the front. "It takes a fair bit to make the trip between here and the Farm. We travel in shifts, and on my way back, I expect to meet Dorie and Cricket. You know them Bill."

Bill nodded at this. Dorie and Cricket were the other two regulars from Abbey Farm that Bill commonly dealt with. Between Cat Jim and those two, there were representatives of the Farm at Bill's place about a week out of every other month, except sometimes in deep winter.

Jim started again. "Well, after Dor and Cricket get back up to the Farm next, it will be my turn again. That's when Tube and I will go back together.

When we get back up, the Farm battens down until March. We'll concentrate on inside crafts, like tanning, forging," Jim looked over at Bill, "and, of course the brewing."

Bill went back to the grill smiling. Jim raised his voice soBill would hear him through the serving window.

"Thing is, I won't be back down until the snow breaks, April, or May maybe." He looked over at Tuba. "That means you'll be out of town for awhile, maybe four months."

Bill had gone back behind the counter to put the food he had made for the fuel men onto plates. He came back now, carrying two steaming portions, each with a scramble of eggs, a chicken haunch and a pile of fried potatoes. "I'll keep your house locked up, Tuba, but things will be tough here without you to lend a hand."

Jim nodded, "I expected as much, Bill, I know how much the boy does around here. So, when I come down to fetch him, I'll bring down an extra load of stock, a third keg and some more meat. Candles, whatever we can spare you for the season. We'll bring another package on our return, and by then Tuba here will know the makings of all of it. How is that for trade?"

Bill took the plates from the bar, put them on a tray, and started for the door. As he pulled the jingling door open, he looked back at the two of them. "It all sounds fine to me now, but come the snows, we'll see how keen a deal it all is." He sounded tired.

Bill looked over at the boy, "You've lived with me a long time Tuba, I'll miss having you around." and with that Bill left to bring the fuel traders their breakfast.

CAT AND TUBA
SHARE A SMOKE

Tuba and Jim had been passing the joint, and now it was coming to a stubby end. Jim crushed it and took up the other carefully rolled tube of tobacco that Rico had traded to him earlier. "Could you get us another coffee, kid?" asked Jim, fishing for his lighter.

"Yeah, Jim, you want honeycomb this time?" Tuba asked. He liked honeycomb in his coffee, but it was a rarity, so he didn't take it out for every breakfast. Today though, between the pot and the offer to finally go up to the Farm with Jim, Tuba was in a celebratory mood. He poured the two cups and broke a chunk of oozing comb into his own.

Jim smiled "None for me, keep what Bill's got. We have bees up at the farm Tuba, likely asleep when you'll get up there though. We'll have honey all summer bud, you just wait."

Tuba brought the coffee back to the bar and sat next to Jim. Jim puffed lazily on the cigarette; the blue smoke lit by bands of noon-time sunlight as it swirled to the ceiling.

"How long have you been here now Tuba?" Jim mused. "I don't remember a time that you weren't about."

Tuba looked out the front windows and into the Yard, Bill was helping the woebegone settlers rig their mules to their caravan, which looked like it finally might be ready to make it back out onto the highway.

"Been here with Bill my whole life." said the boy absently, "Never been anywhere else."

Outside the window the caravan, a sort of wagon cobbled together from a pickup truck with the cab's top sawn off, rolled toward the gate, pulled by the mules Tuba had cared for over the past few days.

Bill was walking back toward the door, wiping sweat from his brow. "I suppose I've been here since forever, now that I think about it," he said, "Bill doesn't talk about it much."

Bill came back in just then and noted the two of them watching him come through the door. "Yeah? What'd I do this time?" The big man laughed.

"Ha, it was nothing, Bill." said Jim. "Tuba and I were just musing on how he came to be here with you. He says he doesn't know the story. I dunno, sounds like a good one, eh?"

Bill stopped behind the counter, he looked at the tile, its age made clear in a thousand fine cracks beneath yellowing glaze. "Well now." he began slowly, "That is a tale." The big man looked back up at Jim and Tuba, sitting with their coffee. Their mild, stoned faces smiled back at him in placid expectation. "I guess now is as good a time as any." he sighed. "Let me get a cup."

When Bill returned, he took up a stool across the bar from the two men, hauling it from beneath a cook surface on the service side of the counter.

"Got another of those joints, Jim?" Bill asked. "This will be heavy remembering."

Jim drew out the small box he had gotten from Rico, and lit another joint. He spun the lighter with a small flourish and handed the jay to Bill, who drew deeply before beginning. "Well, I was born on a little farm. I suppose it must've been something like yours, Jim. Down in a place called Castle Rock. You'll pardon me when I say that we were a bit less sophisticated than your abbey."

Jim nodded, the little cigarette made its rounds, and Bill began again.

"Well, I left when I wasn't much older than you are, Tuba. When I was about twelve, the green cough swept through our colony. We lost maybe half of our number, my parents among them." The big man chuffed and took a sip of his coffee.

Jim broke in, "A friend at the Abbey, Timothy, brews an ale that treats Greencough." He said. "Some of it, at any rate."

Bill cleared his throat again before continuing, "Well, we had no such ale at my colony, and I was young enough to think Greencough a plague one couldn't cure. The end of it was that I lived with one of the farmwives that had lost her own kin. Mara was her name. She was good enough to me, she treated me me good I mean. I, uh, I learned to cook." Bill looked around and shrugged. "Seems I found my element." He said.

"After I left, when I was seventeen or so, I came north to Denver. I was sure that the big city would have need of a rough guy like me. After all I had done, I thought maybe there was some opportunity to be had where the raider gangs met up." Bill laughed then, "I was right, sure, but boy was I stupid."

BILL GETS A JOB

"See," Bill began, after refilling his coffee cup. "My ideas came from traveler stories and fireside bullshit. I thought Denver would be some sort of bastion of society. I thought they'd be trying to rebuild, right?" The big man snorted. "Wow, was I wrong. Right too, in a way, but I'll get to that."

The joint was finished, but neither Jim nor Tuba was in a jovial mood, both were rapt, hanging on Bill's story. Bill got up, went to the back of his kitchen and returned with a bag of walnuts. The gruff man poured these into a large bowl, then, rummaging in a bin of tools beneath the counter he garnished them with pliers, placed the bowl on the counter, and continued. "Look, I was young, seventeen years old, and no parents at home to steer me away." He looked meaningfully at Tuba, who nodded reassuringly to the old man. A reminder that he didn't know any parents beyond Bill.

"Pretty quickly I fell in with a crew of punks that were affiliated with some very powerful people. These guys I knew weren't much, but their allies ran with a gang called the Buffalo Boys." Bill paused long enough to take another drink of his coffee and crack three or four walnuts onto the counter before beginning again. "The Buffalo Boys were huge."

"Our little gang didn't do too much. We'd hold up travelers going over the mountains, shake 'em down for the good stuff. We'd usually let them go, though. Once in a while we went down to the foothill settlements and liberated some goods, fuel and meat mostly, but we weren't usually killing too many folks." Jim and Tuba had forgotten their breakfasts for the moment, listening and sipping at their coffees.

"Our crew had scored this little four-wheeler, a gas car. We rarely had fuel for it, but it had a book and, kids, I can read. So, I got to be the guy that drove the four-wheeler. We could tow a bunch more stuff with that thing running, but come on, who has gas anymore? I probably only drove that thing a dozen times in two years. The basics would sure come in handy later though. In the end? We hoped we would get a name for ourselves, right? So that the Denver gangs would notice us and buy us in. In particular, the guys I ran with favored those Buffalo Boys, and eventually they would be who we hooked up with." Bill shifted on his stool and went on.

"See, the B Boys owned whole tracts of the old city itself. Lock stock and barrel, right? Ground level was all B-Boy guards, and first few floors nothing but drinking halls, whoring, and gambling rooms. Money, that. To a cadre of unfulfilled commune dregs, it was a ticket to the big time. The long and short of it being that less than a month or so into living in the city I ended up in debt to the B Boys myself. Little things here and there, they add up when you're young and foolish. It's funny how fast your 'friends' disappear when you're in hock to a mob."

"Luckily for me, this mob needed more cooks. People who knew how to run a kitchen well enough to feed all of the customers that the Buffalo gang were finding themselves in charge of. They were pretty overwhelmed by the transition from petty criminals to something like a proper business, something that likely saved my scrawny neck at the time."

"Thanks to my surrogate mother, I was savvy enough in the cook-room to schmooze myself into running one of the kitchens and earning a reasonable wage. Sure the B Boys were sharks, and charged me for the room upstairs, and the food I ate, and any other thing I could take advantage of. Still, I made back my debt, just very, very slowly."

KING OF THE FOURTH FLOOR KITCHEN

T he Buffalo Boys held a whole swath of lower downtown. They had the buildings lashed together up top with cat-walks and bridges and shit, the alleys between all walled up and barricaded. All those blocks of shops and condos built to-gether into a massive block of drug-selling, arms-dealing, exploit-ation and general dirty pleasure."

"I ended up in a big red and black skyscraper in the north part of what used to be downtown. It had a funny ridge at the top you could see from miles away, like a loaf of bread turned on its side, sort of. I was working in that tower for four, maybe five years when the shit finally got really bad. The fourth- floor kitchen was my house, and what I said went, pretty much. I had a bunk, a few shelves, some outfits, random shit, you know. I could go to the bars and the dancehalls on the off hours, as long as I had some-one minding the kitchen just in case. I did alright, and as long as I didn't go nuts in the casino or binge on B-Boy liquor I could live comfortable."

"I saw a lot from my post as cook though. You'd be surprised how much talk can slip in between a request for a late night sandwich and the time I fry up the chips they inevitably want with the damn thing."

"I heard all of the gossip, I did well, turned my head at the more unsavory things I was exposed to. I was just trying to get by, y'know? And well, I saw a lot of folks those days, heard a lot of things. Unfortunately I didn't hear everything."

"Still, I didn't just cook the food. A lot of the time I had to run it upstairs to the girls in the rooms, or downstairs to the clients at the bars, whatever. I didn't always have help in the kitchens, but I always had orders."

Bill ate a few walnuts, and pushed the bowl back toward Jim and Tuba before continuing. "I can't pretend I was always a good guy, those years..." he trailed off and then continued. "I did what I could to make ends, right? I mean, hell, in the end it's all a part of how you came to be here, kid." Bill took a slug of his coffee, finishing the cup, before he went on with his story.

"They had girls working on the third, fifth, and sixth floors that I knew about. Working girls, you follow."

Bill seemed flustered; he looked over at Tuba and Jim, who nodded sagely together.

"Well, the kitchen and laundries and shit were all on the fourth, right in the middle. Sometimes I had to be party to some unpleasantness. Sometimes I'd happen on a girl in trouble, and have to intervene." Bill coughed. "More often though, I'd come up on the aftermath and have to help clean up."

"More than once I've muscled a fellow out a fire escape, into the black. Messy business, but they always had it coming."

"After a while though, my goals got real simple. I wanted to pay out the 'Boys and get my move on. Sure, I came around sniffing for work when I was young, but when it gets down to it, kids, after a while a guy wants to settle down. That was no place for that.

It is loud and cruel in the city, just too much noise and bluster and sad, sad people. I thought I'd go north, maybe all the way to Wyoming if I had to, just as far as I needed to set up my own kip, away from the endless carnival that gang had turned their half of Denver into. Wouldn't you guess it was the very day I had saved enough scratch to buy them out, and get my own. Well, that's when it all turned into a raging shitstorm."

BILL AND JUMBO

"So I guess I met this guy Jumbo just a few weeks after I was hired on. He came on as a door bouncer at the ground floor of the building, and anyone could guess why. Jumbo was a real big boy, he just let his size do the talking for him and got the ground floor job."

"I met him at chow on his first shift. I was serving over the steam table, as usual. And when he came through the door the whole hall noticed, a kinda hush settled in y'know? I mean the guy barely fit through the mess hall door, he had to have been seven feet tall."

Bill looked over the bar at Tuba, already a lanky six and a half foot at only sixteen.

"All the boys called him Jumbo, I guess 'cos of his size, and he was a big man. I found out later that no one understood his actual name, but I'll get to that. That first day, he asked me for a few extra biscuits, and kids, I gave them to him. Shit, I gave him extra honey and gravy too, anyone could use the favor of a guy that size. In some time, though, I came to know him. He became more than just that big-ass black man at the door. Sure, he was still an imposing brute on the job, but a nice enough guy over coffee, once you knew him."

"We used to share smokes now and then, when I'd step out into the street for the moment. We'd talk shit about the girls working the building, or joke about odds on this or that deadbeat hustler making enough scratch to come in on any given night. Mine was a workman's kitchen, I didn't serve customers, I fed the whores, right? So, anyway, he'd come up after his shifts for a couple of drinks somewhere out of the noise of the gambling and the floor shows and we'd just talk and talk."

"He taught me Santa Fe Rummy on one of those nights in the winter. The snow was so high that the first two floors were snowed in solid for three days before the B Boys could dig them out. They had a crew of poor motherfuckers out there day and night, shoveling pathways and shit all over. When they got them made though, the folks came right back. Tramping the little hallways the B Boys had cut into the snow to the one warm place in Denver. It was marketing genius."

"See, sometime before I showed up, the founders of the Denver Buffalo Boys had stolen themselves the means to make some real power. And no bullshit, these guys had four diesel-electric locomotives tied up right at the base of the building. How they got them there I have no fucking clue, but what most folks didn't know about the that bigassed Quonset hut at the base of the building was that those monster engines sat in there, pumping heat and light and magic-fucking-fingers into the building at the whim of the big boys up top.

Not even all of my shit was propane, I had electric water heat for one, and the big cold chest for all the perishable foods was electric too. I knew it was there, but it was a kind of magic to me. I didn't ask and no one was talking, y'know?"

"So, that winter, the B Boys had heat and they made roads that led right up to their door. Did they dig out the neighboring gangs? Fuck no, didn't even throw 'em a shovel. Pretty soon everyone's coming down to our buildings, funneled down into the trenches and led right up to the doors of the nice, warm casinos. Genius."

"Well, so, anyway, this one night, I go out for a smoke and Jumbo's got some serious look on his face, real intent. I ask him how he's doin', what's the word on the street tonight, right? Same old bullshit." Bill stood up behind the counter and began to pace, after a few steps he produced a dingy rag from his apron and begins slowly mopping the stainless counter in front of them, though really, it was already clean.

"But it ain't the same old bullshit, not tonight. Jumbo is all hushed like, looking around, trying to talk to me out of the side of his mouth, looking one way and talking the other. Like, I can tell he's nervous, right?"

"And all at once, he just lays it on me smooth how he's thinking of getting out, maybe soon, and there's something else, right? Something he isn't saying. I ask him about it. I tell him I'm on the inside, that I'd know if there was heavy shit brewing. But that was bullshit really, I was just trying to make him relax and give me more details. Maybe I can do something to help, right? But he doesn't bite, doesn't want to talk. Tells me to hit him up when he comes up for a drink around midnight. I say OK and start back up to the kitchen on four, but on the way, just around floor two, I run into one of the bosses' goons, a jerk named Chekout."

CHEKOUT TIME

"Chekout was a thug in general that did bouncer work for our mutual employers. He liked to walk around with his shirt-off, I guess to show off his shitty tattoos, like he had something to be proud of. Sure, the guy was pumped, but the yards of badly drawn skulls, whores' names, and what I guess were supposed to be dragons scrawled all over him were a little uninspiring. Maybe it would have looked nicer with some color, but I doubt it."

"So anyway, Chekout's looking for me, right? He starts in about what Jumbo was talking about. Starts asking me questions about if he's got a regular girl, says the bosses know we chum around.

That's when I see that he's got my keys in his hand, the kitchen keys – the keys to my room. He says the bosses want to talk to me, like now, like before I go back upstairs, which means someone else is doing the late shift dinner at this point, 'cause if I don't get back up there it ain't happenin'. I'm wondering what's going on with my crew, right? Like what the fuck are they up to with the kitchen locked? And all I can think is that they've discovered the holdout I'd been saving to buy them out, and I'm about to get tossed or beaten up, right? But no, I'm about to find out that it's worse than that, way."

"So, I'd seen Chekout fight, he'd be downstairs in the meat rings at least once a month. Kickbacks and ring prizes were a nice little bonus for him. And, yeah, I'm a fairly big dude, but that mother-fucker was insane, and I have never been a prize fighter, even then. So I follow this guy up the hall to the back stairs."

"I'm dreading the trip up, see, 'cause the bosses are on forty, and that's a long assfucking hike. But Chekout walks right past the door, right? And he goes into the back, into the dark halls by the old elevators."

"The elevators, right? Seriously, I hadn't ever seen them used, didn't know they even worked! No-one uses the elevators, certainly no clients. As far as I knew they were empty shafts, long, hard ladders to the top. The halls down at the end were damned dark, but Chekout pulled a little crank light from his belt and wound it up, and when he flicked the switch the bunch of little lights at the front made it bright as day."

"That's a nice little trick." I said, about the crank light, but Chekout only chuckled and told me to keep up. We went into the quiet and the dark, and Chekout walks right up to the bank of elevators, and sticks a little key into the panel at the side, and no shit, that whole panel just lights up."

Tuba laughed and said "What?! What do you mean lights up? No one's got fuel to run a generator for an old world tower!"

Bill nodded and put his hand out toward Tuba, "Every button on the panel, kid. I swear to you. Looked like some magician had touched the thing with his wand. Fifty lights, more even, and they all lit right up. It's those train engines, somehow they keep those monsters fed." Bill shook his head at this, and said "Maybe it's time for a beer."

Bill went into the back and came back with a large brown bottle that Tuba recognized as one of the magnums come down from Abbey Farm. He set the bottle on the bar and continued.

"So the doors slide open and this little room behind 'em had an electric light at the top, it was on too, that sort of glow that no oil flame ever looks like. We went in, and the doors slid closed all by themselves, all creepy and loud."

"A moment later I felt the little chamber rise, and my stomach fell right out of me as we went up. The bosses' rooms were on forty, and we were locked together in that little room for what seemed like an hour while my stomach did little flip-flops on the floor."

"I tried instead to focus on the posters on the elevator wall. There was one on each, in a silvery sort of frame and under a dull sheet of plastic. Thing is, they had lights behind 'em or something because they had a glow that lit up the little room we were in. One had a girl in a swimsuit by a pool of sparkly clear water. One had a dish with some greens, a bunch of little squiggly pink things and a cut of meat on a plate. Looked mighty good to me, looked like beef, I remember thinking. Ain't nothing been served up all fancy like that since before I was born, let me tell you."

Bill turned and blew the cork from the bottle with a loud pop. He pulled long from the big bottle and wiped his beard with the back of his hand before he continued.

"We finally get to the top and Chekout just sort of pushes me into this big room and splits, those silver doors slip shut, and he's hanging out with the swimming pool girl and the beef dinner."

"Now I didn't talk to the bosses where I was at in the gang, not much at all. I mean, yeah, I know the lieutenants, people like Chekout, some less worthless, but I don't know these upstairs cats from anyone else, right?"

"And so, these rooms are crazy nice, on top of it all. This place looked just like it must have when it was built, better even, since these dudes had been looting Denver for longer than I'd been alive."

"And then I'm standing there in this hallway, like a dick, and no one's coming to talk to me, right?"

"I remember that there were these suits of armor that had little plaques in front of 'em. I read one, and it said they were from the "Island nation of Japan". It had a year on it, thirteen-thirty-four. It was already ancient when the old worlders put it in the museum that the B Boys must have raided to bring it there."

Bill laughed ruefully before continuing. "I remember wondering if the B Boy armories built their scrap and tire designs based on these old works of art. So, while I'm looking at this old stuff and feeling self- conscious a couple doors open and out comes what I can only assume is the boss. Only it's not, it's just another one of their guys. Turns out there isn't a boss so much as there are the bosses, a bunch of guys, and I'm only just about to find that out."

A DRINK WITH
THE BOSSES

"This guy that comes out is about my age, dressed nice, in an old world sort of outfit that had a bunch of buttons down the front and a little scarf around his neck. He was confident enough that I would have sworn he was a boss, and he was, just not the boss. He sticks his hand out and I guess I took it, and he kinda pulls me along as he shakes it and says something about having drinks in the other room with the 'Old Boys'."

"So, the Old Boys were waiting for me at the end of this long table in a room just off the hall there.

There were windows all along the wall, and I could see out farther than I've ever seen anywhere off of the mountain. I'll never forget that view. I remember that there was a fire burning way out there in the darkness, a big fire."

"One of the guys at the table, much older than I was, pointed to a thick square bottle and said to me "Hey yo, Bill, have a drink. Sit on down here and tell us what you know about why we've brought you on up." And I nodded at him, sort of dumbly and told him that I really couldn't. And he started going on. He said "Honestly we hadn't heard shit about you until yesterday, but you've been here a few years, am I right?"

I told him that was so and he starts asking me about the circles that I hung around with, starts asking me how often I see the downstairs door guard.

That's when I figured out that he's talking about Jumbo. Except he keeps calling him mister Djambo, so I'm kinda confused, right? And he keeps mentioning someone else too; someone I don't know named Adilah."

"Now I didn't play with the Buffalo Girls. That was an expensive habit. I've never really been one for whoring anyway, or maybe I'd have put it all together faster. I must have seemed like a straight-up sap to those Old Boys. 'Cause, see, Adilah was a popular girl as it turned out, she had been sort of a star in one of the other buildings, a dancer. And it was starting to sound like Adilah had taken ill, or to be really honest, taken pregnant."

"That was some serious shit in its way, if the girl was knocked up they'd charge the momma for the food and care, maybe sell the kid when it got old enough, maybe keep it if it was a girl, but only to put her to work when she got about twelve..." At this he shook his head roughly. "Anyway, wasn't great for the mother or the kid. Not really my problem though, so I was still waiting for the punch line, wondering why I was up here in the penthouse with the bosses, right? I ask them what they want me to tell them about all of this, since I don't know shit. I tell 'em that all I do is make the food, that Jumbo doesn't talk about the girls or nothing like that, that we just talk shit. I guess that was enough because pretty soon they just sorta finished up and started talking to each other, ignoring me, right? A guy I didn't know walked me to the stairwell and told me to go on back to my kitchen, so I started down the stairs. Took for-fucking-ever to get back down to four, and when I did, I was in for even more surprises."

TURNED OUT

"**M**y room at the back of the kitchen was fucking wrecked. All my stuff turned upside down, shit thrown everywhere. Worst, though? Whoever had turned me out had found my stash. All that I had put away to buy myself out, a fat sack of B Boys gambling chips, fucking years of saving up. I was so pissed. I mean, I had nothing to do with this shit, and here I was on watch under the big boys, fucked out of my freedom. I looked around for a minute and I saw the claw hammer that I kept in the tool bin laying amongst the wreckage of my life. So, I picked it up and went looking for answers. Man, I was down to kick an ass."

"I go out to the stairs, I'm looking to find out who the fuck tossed my room. I was so mad I wasn't even thinking about what might have been going on with Jumbo, and I didn't give a shit about this Adilah chick, so I wasn't at all prepared for what I was about to run into.

I go slamming into the stairwell and I'm halfway down the flight when I realize that Jumbo and Chekout are right in front of me on the landing. They hadn't seen me yet, which is, I'm sure, why my ass is still alive."

"Jumbo is yelling at Chekout, and I hear him say something about getting the fuck out and to just let him go, but Chekout is having none of it. He's saying Jumbo is gonna pay for what he did, and that's when I see the gun. A fucking gun, right? A gun back then was crazy shit. Bullets ain't cheap, know what I'm saying? A gun comes out, you know it's business time."

"So anyway, Chekout's got this little rifle, this wide bore thing with a stubby barrel and a little wooden stock tucked under his elbow. He's all pointing it at Jumbo and Jumbo is turning away from him. All in slow motion, I saw Jumbo's other arm all wrapped up in cloth, like he tied it all up in blankets and he's got his free arm up between his face and the gun, like it's gonna do anything against that fuckin' beast. So I did what I guess anyone would do for a friend, I smacked Chekout upside the head with that claw hammer and took that asshole down."

"I can't even describe the look on Chekout's face when I hit him with the hammer. I bet he went to God's gate not even knowing what happened. I whacked him good and solid right about the top of his head and he just fell like a sack of loose rocks. The hammer kind of stuck and pulled out of my hand when he fell away from me.

He was bleeding everywhere; I remember watching as he hit the concrete landing, seeing the wave of gambling chips spill out of his pockets and spin across the floor.

I hadn't ever killed anyone with such intent before, right? Like I had robbed people sure, even been there when people got shot, but this made me kinda sick. Like I didn't puke, but I was sorta dizzy, right? And there was this wailing, like a siren echoing through the stairwell, it hurt my head, I couldn't place it." "I grabbed up Chekout's gun and turned to ask Jumbo what the fuck was happening.

That's when I saw that he was all splashed in blood. I wondered if he was hurt, and I looked again at his arm, all swaddled up in blankets, but it wasn't his arm, those blankets were wrapped around a fuckin' baby."

"Jumbo was alright, the blood wasn't his and this kid was wailing loudly enough to convince me that it wasn't his blood either. Jumbo shook my arm and we started down the stairs. "Damn it all, bro," he said, "You weren't supposed to get drug into this." The baby was still screaming. I was all reeling with the idea that I had murdered Chekout in a split second. What the fuck were we even gonna do, right?"

THE SHIT IS IN
THE WIND

"So, Jumbo is leading me downstairs. I ask him what the fuck, right? And he stops at the door to the back courtyard and says "They fucking killed her, Bill." I remember clear as day. He said "They beat her to fucking death, can you believe that shit? I held her in my arms!" He was crying and I don't think I'd ever seen a grown up man cry before that minute. I felt for my friend, and boys, let me tell you I was pissed off too. But even more compelling was the fact that I had just put down Chekout in the stairwell and that wasn't going to go unnoticed for long.

I had to get out just as surely as my buddy did, and the baby? I didn't even know what we were gonna do about that. I hadn't seen a baby since I had left the mountain, and I wasn't all that involved in child rearin' there either. Anyway, I didn't know it yet, but Jumbo had a plan."

"We went out in to the back courtyard, and there are those big-ass quonset huts out there, like hangars from one of the old airports. Jumbo motions that I should follow him and his loud-ass baby, who was just finally starting to quiet down a little bit."

Bill looked to Tuba at this and said "Kid, you nearly got us killed about fifteen times that night. But anyway, Jumbo pulls out this key ring with a bunch of brass on it and unlocks the place and we go in, right? And then there are the train engines, all peeling black and yellow. Only you can't see all four of 'em at once 'cause they're so fucking big, right?

They took up most of the space in there. On two sets of rails side by side. Train engines as big as those containers outside, boys, they made a guy feel tiny. We went right down the space between them, it was, like, maybe three feet wide, all chunky gravel. Two of those engines were running, too. They made this thunderous rumbling, you could feel it in your balls." Bill chuckled a bit and pulled on the beer.

"Jumbo seemed to know right where we were going, so I just jogged along behind him. I remember wondering when everybody was gonna figure out what was going on and come after us, but right then it was still quiet." He laughed again, "I mean aside from the train engines. They were all that we could hear aside from the gravel under our feet. Even the baby stayed miraculously quiet for most of the way."

"Jumbo hustled us along until we reached the far end of the building, where there was a small parking lot, the huge doors open to the night. A few cars and bikes stood next to one of those silver tanker trucks in the parking area, and a pair of guards stood there with their backs to us outside the big door. They were facing outward, talking about something, I guess. So, I look over at Jumbo to see what his plan is, and he's already moving toward that truck.

I could hardly ask him what he was up to without making a noise that the guards might hear, so I just padded along behind him up to the cab. Luckily, the baby kept quiet and we were able to put the body of the truck between us and the guards when we approached the driver's side door. Jumbo reached right up and unlocked it, he had the damn key."

A SHINY, WHITE TRUCK

"**I** couldn't believe what I was looking at. This truck was shiny and clean like it had been built just last week, rather than gods-only-know how long ago. I mean it was polished! The lights were shining off of the thing's white paint, practically sparkling. It was pretty incredible. I remember wondering what sad fool had to wash and shine that monster and thinking that was a stupid thing to think about when the biggest gang in Denver was about to kill you." Bill laughed. "We, uh, left that truck in considerably worse shape than we found it."

He chuckled a moment further before continuing. "But I'll get to that. Anyway, Djambo has already pulled open the door and is behind me trying to push me up into the cab with his one free hand. I climb in and slide over to the other seat, it smelled like leather and tobacco inside. I remember there was a wrinkly yellow paper cutout of a tree hanging from the sticks next to the wheel, and a kind of picture of a bulldog on the wheel itself. Djambo got in and put the baby between us, and I think that's about when the guys at the back door started to figure out that something wasn't right. They started shouting at us up in the truck, and then the engine comes alive and Djambo laid on the horn, I guess just to do it, I don't know, really. It was damn loud in that garage, though.

He pushed the pedal and the truck sort of lurched forward. I was kind of in shock, I guess, stunned or something. I hadn't ever been in such a big truck. Anyway, I lost track of where the guard guys had gotten to, and before I could figure it out, the door next to me opened and one of them was riding right there on the metal step, reaching in to grab me. He caught me by the shoulder and down I went, right out the door and into the concrete, face first."

Bill's hand went to his brow, lingering over an old scar only just visible there.

"I guess I sort of blacked out or something, because the next thing I knew Djambo was helping me up. I couldn't hear a goddamn thing but the ringing I my ears. My vision went all blurry. Man, I was fucked.

Djambo is yelling at me to get up, that we gotta go, and I realize that there's this terrible screaming, and I remember the baby, and where we are and what's going on, and I get up. The truck was still running, Djambo had stopped it from rolling away before he got out. He was helping me back to the cab, and that's when I noticed the blood.

There was kind of a lot of it, all streaked down the side of the truck. I followed it down to the floor and the guy that had pulled me out of the truck was laying there, half under the cab. It looked like he had maybe hit his head on the side of the truck a couple times. I gotta admit I was a little fuzzy, and I didn't have a lot of time to look, Djambo helped me into the truck then ran around the front where I couldn't see him and climbed in the driver's side. You were still right there between us on the seat. Djambo had sort of tied you in with the belt, and I was putting on my own when he got back in.

When he opened the door, I saw the other guard on the floor outside the door, and I'm pretty sure he was dead too. Djambo put a god-awfully large revolver on the dash and was telling me to hold the fuck on, but my head was still spinning from the faceplant and I think I threw up on my feet before I got the belt fixed. Oh, and the baby was done being quiet. Djambo kept telling him to calm down, that "it was gonna be alright B." Kept saying "Barry, Barry, be cool."

Bill shook his head, remembering. He looked at Tuba. "Djambo looked over you at me and said, "His name is Baritone, Bill, like from Adilah's music." Bill finished the beer in one long pull, wiped his rough beard, and sighed.

HIS NAME IS BARITONE

"Well shit kid, there it is. Your name is Baritone. I guess I just hadn't thought about that night, not all the way through. Not until now. Heheh, I remember thinking that you were loud enough to be a tuba, and I suppose that was what stuck with me."

The boy looked at him, dark eyes far away. "It's cool, Bill. I like Tuba. It's nice to know what my mom would have called me, but you've been my dad my whole life."

Jim nodded, "I've always liked Tuba, it's a good handle." He turned over his empty coffee cup on the counter and seemed to suddenly remember his chicken. He bit into the thickest part and chewed heartily. "Even cold your chicken is the best outside of home, buddy." He said when he had finished.

Bill smiled at this "Thanks for the compliment, Jim. Exactly how many chicken shacks are there from here to Abbey Farm?" at Jim's laugh, he added "I'd just like to know who my competition is."

Jim finished more of the chicken with relish. "My buddy Nick cooks a good bird, but you've got a touch, no doubt about that." He said. "The real question, though, is where you get the coffee."

Tuba piped up at this. "I know that one. It's the Way, they bring it down from up north. I guess they grow it up there and do all the stuff to it so we can cook it here. Everybody coming through here wants it, which is weird. I mean it costs almost as much as fuel."

At this, Bill's countenance darkened. "Yeah. Which I guess brings me back to the story. See, the truck we were busy stealing? It was full of nice, clean biodiesel. Right then I was busy trying to get my addled brainpan unfucked and not at all thinking about how this guy I smoked cigarettes with knew how to drive this big-assed truck. I had thought that we were in a pretty thick part of the city, but Djambo's only gotta slow down to turn down a couple streets before we're on a straightaway. He was watching the side mirror, and he says "If I tell you to drive, we're gonna have to switch places. You think you can get over the kid and get on the wheel here?"

"Now this truck had all kinds of those round meters, 8 of 'em across the driver's side of the dash. There wasn't one of those shifting sticks in the middle either, just this big switch on the front panel for drive gears and neutral and all that. Those, at least, were marked, but the dials were all stuff I couldn't figure out right away, and there was a bunch of switches down the middle panel that I didn't have any idea what were all for.

"This is a nice rig," Djambo says "the nicest I've ever driven. See." and he kinda waved at all the dials and shit "the B Boys kept it all working, so it's point and go, mostly." Anyway, I could hold a wheel straight and there were only three pedals that I could see. I told him that I thought I could do it."

"He looks up from the mirror about then and says, all calm, "Good, then buddy, get ready to." and then he slows us way down and pulls right onto this long, curved bridge down to the interstate, and then there we were rolling down the on-ramp onto wide open '25. Jumbo got us onto the flat part of the road and picked up the revolver off of the dash, then he leans toward me and says "It's time for you to drive."

"We didn't even stop rolling, just slid across each other as quick as we could without sitting flat on you, kid. Then I put the pedal down, Jumbo started rolling down the window with the little crank. The whole truck lurched forward, and ever so slowly, we started picking up speed."

"We actually got going pretty fast before anything bad happened. We had been riding smooth for something like five, six minutes. The road was wide open, there was like nothing on it, except those little concrete barrier walls in the middle. Not a fucking soul out. My heart had slowed down, the baby stopped crying. I remember looking out over the ruins all around us. That city was really big once. You know, before."

PURSUIT

"Djambo's all looking back out the window and he says, "Things are gonna get loud here in a second, Bill. You just be cool and keep this bitch straight. When they start shooting at us, and they will, keep that wheel steady or we'll roll right the fuck over and that will be the end of it."

"So I'm holding tight, and trying to keep the speed on without vibrating our shit apart, and Djambo leans out the window and fires the gun a couple of times, like toward the back of the truck." Bill made like he was leaning out a window. He pointed at Tuba, "You just lost it and started squalling again.

I must have still been kinda out of it, 'cause I about jumped out of my skin and came right back to the moment just then. There were motorcycles coming up behind us. I told 'jambo, but he was already nodding. He already had his head back in the cabin, too."

"More than you think, bro." He told me, "At least two bikes, but they've got a car or truck too, can't tell
yet."

"I looked back at my mirror and I could see one of the bikes coming alongside out of my blind spot. It was all spindly, just the frame and the engine and a big headlight. Behind that light I could see a shadow of a rider.

The guy had one hand off of the handlebars and was kind of standing up on the pegs. I could feel a bunch of little jolts through the wheel, and I was pretty sure that motorbike guy was shooting at us."

Bill barked a short laugh through his beard.

"That was just about terrifying. I remember thinking, 'My gods this tanker is full of gas, it's gonna blow the fuck up!' and 'He's going to shoot me!' all at the same time. I pushed myself back against the seat as hard as I could. Djambo started firing that gun again, three, four times, then he was back in the cab and I could hear him swearing. He'd burned his leg reloading the gun." Bill's voice rose, unsteady. "And when I turned to look back into my mirror that guy on the motorbike was right outside my window, pointing this long pistol right at me. The thing was absurdly big, or maybe that was just my memory playing tricks. I couldn't see the guy's face, he was wearing one of those round all over helmets with a black, reflective, visor thing."

Bill sighed and took a deep breath. "Well, I panicked, but I remembered Djambo telling me not to jerk the wheel or we'd roll over. So, I squished myself back into the seat and pushed on the gas pedal a little bit and let the wheel kind of drift to the left, toward that biker. He was already shooting, I think. I mean he must have been, but I don't remember hearing the shots. My ears were already ringing pretty bad.

Djambo's revolver was going again but I didn't dare lean forward to look at him. The window beside me exploded across my lap, there was glass flying all over the cab. I was holding that wheel so damn tight my fingers went numb."

Bill got up, turned to the coffee urn behind him and pumped himself another cup of coffee. His hands shook as he turned back to the bar. Cat Jim had abandoned the chicken bone, now thoroughly gnawed, to the edge of his plate. He was scraping the last of his cold potatoes into a greasy pile with the edge of his fork. Tuba just sat wide-eyed, listening. He held his empty cup out and Bill swapped him his full one for the empty, he looked over at Cat, who just shook his head, chewing the last of his potatoes.

When he had filled the second cup with coffee and come back to the bar, Bill continued. "I, um, well, the truck inched over toward the left side of the interstate, where the dividers usually were. They'd been broken out to make the two-lane part we were on into like four lanes, see? And there was one of those green overhead signs coming up, I remember. It said 'Boulder: Exit Only' and had arrows pointing at the part of the road we were riding on. I revved the engine and the bike fell back a little, so I could see him in the mirror again. He was trying to back off of the truck, but I wasn't going to let him. So, I just took my foot off the gas for a second and all of a sudden he's right back up at my window, pointing that damn gun at us. I swear I was sprayed with powder, or that bullet missed my face by an inch. I saw a bunch of flashes from that side, he must have been just blasting away.

We were coming up on a section of the road where those concrete rails were unbroken. I saw them coming up just three or four feet to the left. I leaned into the wheel and gunned the engine and that bike went right over." Bill laughed nervously. "I knew because his headlight did this crazy up-end thing. I don't know if he hit the rail or if he didn't see the drop-off. It happened so fast. Right as we went under that sign. Maybe not a boulder, but that guy sure did exit." Bill laughed again, shaking his head.

"By some miracle, the guy hadn't hit the windshield when he was shooting at us. There were holes in the dash, in the goddamn roof, even in the frame by the window, but the windshield was still whole. I figured I should get back over toward the middle of the road. Had I been able to think about it at the time, I would have wondered how all the wrecks and junk and shit I saw off the edges of the pavement got moved there, but I was way too busy trying not to die. 'Jambo was sitting back in the cab, and his window was open too, but I couldn't tell if it was down or broken. There was glass all over us. He was leaned back and just kind of breathing, holding the gun in front of him like he was resting or praying or something. In my mirror I saw lights that meant there was someone behind us, but the trailer blocked out what they were driving."

Bill coughed and took a sip of his coffee, toyed with a walnut on the counter. "I ask Djambo what's up, I'm like 'Check the baby, man, and what happened to the other bike?' going on and on, and he looks at me and says, "I shot that fucker in the face." Then he looks down at you and brushed off some little glass chunks and says "baby's good."

He's all quiet now, solemn like, none of that urgency from earlier and I wonder if he's just now figuring out how thoroughly fucked we are." Bill barked his short laugh again.

"So, I ask him what's the plan? And he says this is it. This is the plan, get out of Denver, head north, that's all. So I ask him, then what? But he's just shaking his head. Says we have to get out first, and as long as those guys are on our ass, we're not out. Then he says "Shit" and sits forward all of a sudden, says "They've got more bikes." And then he checks the pistol and puts a couple more rounds in."

"Me, I tried to ease on the gas pedal, get more speed, but every time I get to about sixty the truck sets up a little side to side shimmy that I really didn't like. So, I start kinda sliding slowly back over to the left, so there's no room between me and the edge of the road. I don't like getting shot at. Then they were there, that fast, right

48

outside the window."

"I'm squishing myself back into the seat as far as I can get, and 'Jambo is too, only he's got his arm out the window and all I can hear is guns and engines and the baby. I remember putting my right hand over your face, kid. Tried to cover your ears, it was so loud. So, I only had my left hand on the wheel and we're just barely missing the divider on my side. If I hadn't gotten right after that guy went over the barrier, we would've hit that shit square. As it was, I was seriously shocked that we didn't scrape on the concrete."

"This time, though, the guy on my side was paying attention. He went around the divider and was on the other side of it. He must have run out of ammo, though, or pulled off too far from us to waste it, because after one or two stray shots he stopped firing and just rode off on the road toward Boulder.

Then, just ahead of him in the dark I saw movement, like a couple cars with the lights off, pull out from the wreckage. For a half a second I was afraid they would be after us too, and I squashed back into the seat again, waiting for the gunfire. But it didn't come, and I couldn't make out how they planned to get across the dividers anyway, and then we were past them and didn't have much cause to keep worrying about it anymore."

"I was just about to sit up again and look at how Jumbo was doing when I felt the whole truck slide sideways away from me. We were slowly dragging away from that gully at the middle of the road, then it let off for a sec. Jumbo says something like 'ah shit they've got a hook.' And then, wham, again. This time the passenger door just sorta tore open, then fell off onto the road at the end of a chain and hook attached to a truck pulling alongside of us."

"Then 'Jambo had his back to me, and I couldn't see past him. There was a pickupout there, I could hear its engine running high and whiny in comparison to the thunder rolling from beneath our feet. Then, the loudest gunshot I've ever heard. Jumbo flinched back over you, kid, the windshield flexed out and sorta just came apart all over the place.

There was blood on the dashboard, splashed my hands. The wind was screaming around us. I was sure that we were dead, but somehow I just held the wheel straight and kept my foot on the gas. Jumbo looked back at me then, and…"

Bill trailed off and took a ragged breath; he looked out the dirty glass into the sunny day outside before continuing.

"Jumbo looked back at me, the gun was on the floor. He was bracing himself oddly in the truck's doorway.

I could hear them revving the pickup to close again. Jumbo said, 'Take care of my boy, Bill' - and then he just jumped. That was it. Just jumped right out into the night."

I saw the truck fall behind until it was out of sight, next to us I assumed. I put my arm around you kid, and pulled you as close as I could and tried to speed up again. I thought I heard a crash behind us but the mirror had gone with the door and I couldn't see. After that it was just you and me and the wind."

LONG, COLD, RIDE

"Damn, Bill. You never told me this shit." Tuba's voice quavered just a little. "I mean, you said it was complicated but…" "Wasn't a secret." Bill cut him off shortly. "Just never was the right time to tell it." Again, the faraway look out dusty windows. "Not exactly a bedtime story."

Cat broke the silence by clearing his throat. "So that's it then?" He slid his empty plate across the counter, finished. "How'd you land here?"

Bill shrugged. "That was the easy part I guess. It was real hard to miss. See, it's cold. Damn cold. I'm driving a truck I don't know nothing about, with a baby.

Up until then I could count the number of babies I'd held on one hand. I didn't know babies. I was just a whorehouse cook."

Cat Jim laughed and looked around dramatically. "No whores here Bill." Bill smiled thin and tight. "No whores here," He agreed.

"How was it hard to miss?" Tuba asked, softly, from behind his cup.

Bill smiled genuinely then, "It was on fire."

LIGHTS AT JO CORNER

T uba laughed out loud. Cat looked amused. "And you de-
cided to steer towards that?" He chuckled.
"Seems to be my instinct." Bill replied, in a tone that sug-
gested he was resigned to it.
"It was The 'Way." Bill went on. "They were burning a couple of
decade's worth of junk, brush and tumbleweed out of this lot."
And he gestured in an expansive way at the lot out the window.
The lot Tuba had grown up in.

"Could see it for miles." He said. "Flames had to be forty feet
high. 'Got closer you could see all manner of trucks and bikes and
people, like they were making a party of it. That was about when
I remembered I had no idea how to drive, let alone stop a damn
tanker truck. That I had about ten thousand gallons of fuel on my
back." He shook his big head and chuckled then, smiling a little.
"Almost blew the whole thing right there at the end."

Bill smiled and turned toward the big windows. "See, there is that
gully between the big road, and the frontage that the 'Way were on
up ahead."

Tuba nodded, he knew the thing, it ran all along between the
cracked spit of a road running just outside their walls, and the
highway itself. Just where the container wall ended there was the

little 2-laner, then a ditch that became a berm, a little hill, then flattened back out a ways past their wall.

"Well. I watched for it to smooth out a little, like it does right before the overpass there," Bill gestured out toward the road. "And right when it did I hauled the wheel over to try to steer this beast onto the connector, so I could try to stop it in front of this army of fuckers. If anyone was following me still.

Maybe they'd back off, you get me?" Jim and Tuba exchanged a glance and shrugged together.

Bill went on. "Well anyway, it almost worked." He chuckled. "The truck… the truck it sort of groaned and pulled and shuddered and then you and me were on that little connector. I laughed aloud, I bet I shouted. But as I hauled that bigass wheel back over hand-over-hand, that rig just shimmied and bucked like a goddamned mustang and then, real slow like, we started to roll over."

Tuba gasped theatrically. "You tried to kill me when I was just a baby!"

Joe laughed. Bill waved his hands broadly in the air before him.

"You have no idea, kid! I abandoned the wheel altogether and grabbed you with both hands. Seatbelts work, let me tell ya, and that one hung us suspended 4 feet from scrubbing our faces off on that broken road right up until the cab stopped skidding."

"No shit?" said Tuba. "How'd you, I mean how did we get out?" He and Jim both leaned forward at this. Bill's face settled into a smirk and he continued. "Are you kidding? The 'Way didn't waste a minute."

"They were on that wreck before I'd even realized we'd stopped. In that moment I was as confused as the babe in my own arms. The

'Way though? It was like they'd seen this shit a hundred times. And, yeah, it turns out they had." Bill laughed hard then, of a sudden before continuing. "I was naïve. I learned a lot about the Iron Way that night, that week! Changed my life."

"Wait. The wall wasn't out there?" Tuba started suddenly up from his stool and walked to the window, looking out at the wall of steel, varied in hue, streaked with countless seasons of rust. His home. Tuba had thought it had to have stood there forever. "Did the 'Way do that too?"

Bill nodded, looking now over Tuba's shoulder. Noticing how tall the boy was getting. "Sure did, kid. The 'Way gets shit done. They sorted us out, for instance." Tuba turned back to Bill and Jim, "What about the fire? And the truck?"

"Fire was on purpose." Bill answered simply. "They had it under control. They were burning out this lot, all the brush and shit that had gathered. The 'Way were fixing this place up, setting it up to be what it is today.

Turns out they needed to secure a nice open lot like this one down south here. 'Way's from I-80 up north y'know. Anyway, the location was good for their travel stop and after what we had been through, we needed somewhere to rest a bit. It all just kinda lined right up."

Tuba turned away from the window, still taking this in. "What about the Buffalo Boys though? They just gave up on that truck?" Disbelief was plain on the boy's face. Bill barked his short laugh, though. "Oh no, that truck alone might have started a war, if the B-Boy's hadn't already been fighting one. See, the 'Way had been growing along '80 for a decade while I was putzing around in the hills. By the time I joined up with the 'Boy's they were already making their way south down '25. Slow and steady, that's their way."

Bill turned and pointed out the filmy windows toward the big gap in the wall where the seldom closed front gate was. "Thing is, border conflicts ain't exactly the sort of thing a warlord talks to a cook about, right? I had no idea, but we blew past the no man's land north of Denver into Iron Way territory way back where that other cyclist peeled off. And I wouldn't know it for another week maybe, but that shit I saw in the dark out there was an Iron Way long patrol, keeping watch in case the burn up here was drawing any attention."

He paused with a chuff, then continued. "Suppose they didn't know what to make of us, hell on fire out of the city, with enforcers shooting at our backsides. Well, couldn't have looked too bad for you and me. Fact that I managed to not spill that load of biodiesel was probably another card in our hand. Then there was you. It's a rare highwayman slings a baby."

Anything the boy was about to say was lost in the jangling door bells as a couple of large men in denim and studded leather strode in, a gust of warm midday air brought with it a whiff of dust and oil. The first of the Iron Way riders, an older man with a salt and pepper scruff and grey whorls in his black hair strode in. Pale blue chambray was stretched taut over a barrel chest under his road leathers.

He nearly shouted as he pushed through the door "Bill! Goddamn it's been too long. What, a dozen years since I been this far south? You've kept this place lookin' real good!"

The man behind him was younger, maybe only 3 or 4 years Tuba's senior, he was looking around the inside of the place and especially at Bill with a sort of subdued wonder. Tuba wondered what he was thinking of when he looked at the old guy. He was filling with a slow realization that Bill had history with the 'Way that went past free breakfasts and a spot on the tarmac, and that meant so did he.

Bill clasped the other man in a warm hug. "Aron! I was hoping that was your scooter out there. Same ride all these years?" Aron scoffed, "I'd sooner trade out the wife than the Lady, Bill." He laughed then, and the windows shook with the depth of the man's mirth.

Still looking at Bill, Aron cocked his head toward Tuba and Jim. "Your boy's grown straight up. Saw him 'cross the yard this morning, took me a good minute to figure who I was lookin' at!" Aron turned to look at Tuba now, "Remember your Uncle A-Rock? Suppose not, last time I was here you was a tyke. Your Pa got you riding yet?" Tuba shook his head, "I'm more familiar with mules and horses, I guess."

Aron made a scoffing noise. "Horse will hang you up on a branch if she gets her dander up, but you treat a bike right and she'll purr all night. Gods Bill, what're you putting' into this kid's head?" He laughed again, amiably enough. Then went on "Jack-Jack here's just 19, this is his first long ride."

"What's the loop?" asked Bill.

The youth piped up in response, "The 'Way's setting up a toll-station down at the interchange. One more length of road locked down. Keep your eyes peeled and you'll catch Lola as she goes over." "Lola?" asked Tuba and Jim at the same time.

Aron's eyes lit up. "Airship!" The single word a slogan. "Pride and joy of the Iron Way, boys!" He looked back at Bill, "What do ya think the lot's for? Really didn't teach him nothin' at all did ya?" Aron was animated, he spoke with his hands and arms, now he held them wide before him.

"Kid, Lola won us the northwest halfway to the Salt Lake, and she'll give us Denver soon enough. Anyone sees her shadow on the ground better hope they're on the right side of the 'Way." That laugh again. "Shit! Bill, didja even teach the kid to shoot?"

Bill had moved back behind his bar and was making a show of cleaning up the mess of the morning. His answer was short. "No." Tuba was bewildered, why should he know how to shoot?

No one had needed Bill to do more than show the big double-barrel he kept under the counter in his whole life. They didn't even need to worry about any sort of animals inside the wall, even the coyotes stayed out.

"So, you guys charge tolls?" Jim suddenly broke in. "How's that work out for someone like me? I'm a trader along these roads."

Aron looked Jim over. "Yeah? Hail from down south or?" "West." Jim answered quickly, "Up the mountain." Jim was probing, Tuba could tell, and Aron nodded slowly before asking, almost sly "You're from the Abbey aren't ya." Jim nodded back, meeting Aron's eye. "You know about us then."

Aron put out a hand, but Jim didn't take it. Aron shrugged and exhaled dramatically exclaiming "Aw, come on hillbilly! We're the good guys! O' course we know about that fortress farm. We've been keeping a few riders on 7 for a decade or so now. Old Estes, couple nice lakes. We've got some farms up there, cutty like. But If you've ever heard a bike like one of those two out there, that was us."

Jim wasn't convinced. "Lot of trouble on the peak to peak, time to time." He licked his lips. "I mean, we keep the peace on our loop, but I don't recall..." Aron cut him off. "Look kid, I reckon you at what 24? 25?" He paused. Jim only nodded.

Aron went on, "OK, well, we sent someone down that direction a long time ago, before my time. They didn't come back, and we didn't ask any questions. We don't want war. Farthest thing from it. We want trade partners. We're talking alliances kid." He shuffled around for a moment then spat it out. "Shit. Fact is, after I check Jack here in, I was meant to go home that way, see if I could test the waters. They thought a guy my age, alone, might be a little less threatenin'."

Jim relaxed visibly. "No shit?" Aron looked up from his dusty boots and smiled like a child. "No shit, bud." He again held out a hand, and this time Cat Jim took it. "What would you say about me following on with you two? You'll do a lot better showing up at the Farm with me as your sponsor."

Tuba stood back as the two men shook heartily, then Aron said "Sure, but you're on a horse, aren't ya?" Jim laughed. "I'm walking, I have a mule." At this Aron groaned.

"I'll have Jack at the interchange by evening. Then I bet I've got two, maybe three days of service to put in down there. If nothing else, they'll take a day to get my trip report all settled. Then I'm taking a damn day off before I head out again. So, why don't we plan a meet up, something like a week from today?" Jim nodded, "Break a map out, fella, I'll point out a few spots along my way."

TUBA MAKES
A CHOICE

Later that day Jim, his mule fed, packs all secured. struck out for his rendezvous with Aron. The two of them had settled on a small crossroads that long ago had been named Lyons, as the faded green and white sign by the wayside still read. This was where the road Jim was taking home slipped into the foothills and began up into the mountains.

Aron and J.J. had left shortly after Jim and Aron's negotiations. Aron had remained jovial, but Bill's mood had cooled just enough for Tuba to note it. After the visitors were gone, he brought this up. "What was Aron going on about not teaching me anything? You've taught me lots."

Bill had been "taking inventory" of the back of the kitchen since the enforcers had ridden out. At Tuba's question, he came back to the front. "The 'Way raises all their kids together, up north." He began.

"Teach the boys to ride, to shoot, mechanics and similar. Teach the girls mostly domestic shit. Y'know cooking, brewing, tailorin'." He shrugged. "They'd have taken you up north in a heartbeat." He paused and sighed. "Look, though, kid. The last thing your daddy did was make me promise to take care of you. What kind of taking care is signing you up for a life with another gang?"

"But the 'Way isn't a gang," Tuba cut in. "they're something else."

"Oh, they're a gang." Bill returned. "They just have a different set of principles than the type of people that paid my way back when I met your dad. Doesn't make them not similar." Bill's countenanced darkened. "They were pretty keen to take you off my hands, anyway, but I couldn't let that happen. Still, I didn't know shit about babies…" He trailed off, looking off into the wavering haze cast across the asphalt yard.

"Sooooo. To cut the story short, I made a deal with them. After the burn out was done. I would stay on around here and help them fix it up, set up the kitchen, do what I know. More important, though, I convinced them to let me keep you around, raise you here."

"You said you didn't know how, though." Tuba said.

"They sent help, I wasn't alone here for a long time. Think back, Aron was around 'til you were 3 or 4. There were patrols coming and going at all hours. Less traders by a long shot. Back then there was still a lot more fighting out on the highway. Not like now."

"But that's what they do, said it themselves." Tuba nodded at the door where the riders had left a few hours earlier. "That's what The Iron Way is, huh?"

"The dreadful storm after which comes peace." Bill grumbled. "That's what Old Doc used to say.

It's their goal to open the roads again, make it safe to travel. To them, that's how the world is gonna get back on its feet. I…" he paused a moment. "I think it's a good goal, I just don't think your daddy got you out of there to see you grow up to be some other kind of thug. And like 'em or not, that's what most of those guys are Tube. They're thugs. I want more for you."

"I always thought they were the good guys." Tuba began.
Bills voice was soft.

"Even good guys can be thugs. Tuba. Some of us just don't know better. I started to catch on to that idea right about the time I decided we were sticking around and sticking together. At least 'til you were in a place to make that choice for yourself, not find yourself forced into it." Bill paused, sighed, and went on again, "and I guess that's just about now."

"I'm going up to the Abbey with Jim for the spring. We talked about it earlier." Tuba ventured. "That's as far ahead as I've planned in a while, Bill. I'm still thinking through all of that."

Bill just nodded. "Yeah, I figured one day you'd want to go up and see the Farm. It's a nice place, been myself a number of times. You've been there too, just once, when you were hardly walking. Jim and I have talked about you going up for a season before, we were just waiting for you to be a bit older."

"Jim said come springtime, he thought, after the snow." Tuba shivered, remembering the frost on his windowsill that morning. It was going to be a cold one this year.

"Yeah, that's for the best." Bill said, nodding. "It'll be worse up there in the hills." As if to echo his sentiment, the sun fell behind a bank of low grey clouds rolling in off the mountains.

"Storm's coming in." said Tuba. "Wonder if it's gonna blow anyone into the yard." He stood from his stool slowly and put his empty cup on the countertop, turning then toward the door. "I think I'll check if anyone needs help setting up animals in the stable. Did that couple leave? They had horses that might want sheltering. I should see to that." He began toward the door but stopped when Bill spoke again.

"Kid, we got time to figure out how this is gonna work out, but it is gonna work out." Tuba nodded and Bill went on. "and I'll be here when you get back. This will always be your place too."

Tuba turned all the way around then, nodding, "Yeah Bill, I know. And uh, thanks." The boy smiled in a lopsided way "I mean, I love you like a dad, that's what you are to me, but now that I know why? Like how I got here? Thanks again from my other mom and dad, out there. You didn't have to do any of that shit. You could have just left, but you didn't." Tuba shrugged. "Thanks for being a good guy thug."

Bill's chuckle was brief and dark. "Alright, go check on those horses then kid. I'll see you in a few hours if you want dinner." Tuba turned back to the door. Bill went back into the storage room to finish up, as he walked down the dim hall towards the back room, the doorbells jingled behind him and Tuba left for the yard.

Here Ends: *Long, Cold Ride.*
Hope to see you again real soon;
Watch for more Iron Way Stories.